OKKO THE SAND MONSTER

BY ADAM BLADE

ORCHARD

VAREEN

THE ICE CASTLE

THE ICY PLAINS

FREESHOR

CITY OF JENGTOR

WELCOME TO

Collect the special coins in this book. You will earn one gold coin for every chapter you read.

Once you have finished all the chapters, find out what to do with your gold coins at the back of the book.

With special thanks to Tom Easton

For James Waldock

www.beastquest.co.uk

ORCHARD BOOKS
First published in Great Britain in 2016 by The Watts Publishing Group
1 3 5 7 9 10 8 6 4 2

A CIP catalogue record for this book is available from the British Library.

ISBN 978 1 40834 082 0

Printed in Great Britain

The paper and board used in this book are made from wood from responsible sources

Orchard Books
An imprint of Hachette Children's Group
Part of The Watts Publishing Group Limited
Carmelite House, 50 Victoria Embankment, London EC4Y 0DZ

An Hachette UK Company
www.hachette.co.uk
www.hachettechildrens.co.uk

GWILDOR
BORDERLANDS

RTAL

MUDDY LAKE

MANGROVE
SWAMP

DUNES

DESERT

CONTENTS

Do you know the worst thing about so-called heroes? They just don't give up.

Well, villains can be just as stubborn… That pesky boy, Tom, and his lackey, Elenna, may have thwarted our siege of Jengtor, but the battle is not over. There are other prizes to be found throughout my kingdom!

In Gwildor's borderlands lie the four pieces of the Broken Star, a legendary "gift" that fell from the sky many, many years ago. Each piece gives its holder immense power, and whoever brings all four pieces together will be undefeatable!

To obtain each piece, one must find a way past the Beasts which guard them. Kensa and I have tricks up our sleeves – and a head-start on our enemies. With the star in our hands, no one will stop us from reclaiming Gwildor.

And then? Avantia!

Your future ruler,

Emperor Jeng

KENSA'S PORTAL

Tom blinked as he emerged from the cave, his eyes taking a few moments to adjust. Bright light reflected off the snowy mountains that soared a thousand feet into the clouds. Tom turned to see Elenna following him out of the cave, rubbing her side. She slumped down on a rock.

"Are you hurt?" Tom asked.

He knew the fight against Thoron had been bruising for both of them.

"Nothing that a good long rest wouldn't fix," Elenna replied with a rueful grin.

"I wish we could rest," Tom said. "But we must follow Kensa and Jeng. They can't have got far, and if they get their hands on the third fragment of the Broken Star, they could cause untold havoc."

Tom felt guilty about pushing his friend to go on, but they simply couldn't stop now. The wicked sorceress Kensa, along with the treacherous Emperor Jeng of Gwildor, had fled north, to the rarely visited areas of the kingdom.

They sought the four fragments of a fallen comet, known as the Broken Star. Each fragment in isolation had powers that could control the weather – the four combined were thought to be an unstoppable force.

Many years before, to stop the fragments falling into the wrong hands, the Good Witch Clara had placed each fragment with a Good Beast under the instructions to protect them at all costs.

"Don't worry," Elenna said, getting to her feet. "I'm ready for anything."

Tom grinned at her. He knew she wouldn't let him down. Turning, he scanned the craggy mountains surrounding them. Thanks to the power of his golden helmet, Tom's eyesight was sharper than an eagle's.

He saw no sign of their enemies. The area around Vareen was utterly barren. Not a blade of grass broke the landscape. No birds flew, no insects crawled over the rocks. He was about to give up, when…

Wait!

In a deep valley between two distant mountains he saw a telltale flicker of colour and movement amidst the drab colours. "There!" he cried. Now he knew where to look, he focussed on the two villains. Kensa was unmistakeable in her black cloak. Jeng, in his flowing robes, walked

a few feet behind, stumbling and clearly tired.

"So what are we waiting for?" Elenna asked, her voice grim. "Let's get after them."

They jogged side by side, taking a

higher route above the valley. Tom felt blisters forming on his feet, but he knew he couldn't stop. They were gaining on their prey.

"Careful," Elenna panted as Tom sped up, scattering dust and pebbles down the slope. "The stones are unstable."

"We can't let them get away," Tom replied. "They deserve to be in a jail cell, along with their friend, Sanpao the pirate."

"You're not going to be putting anyone in a jail cell if you tumble off the side of this mountain," Elenna pointed out. Even as she said this, Tom's ankle turned on a loose stone. He felt his stomach lurch as he swayed perilously close to the edge of the ridge and the plummeting drop to the knife-sharp rocks below. Elenna was right. He slowed his pace a little, picking his way more carefully through the treacherous rocks.

Turning his attention to Kensa and Jeng again, Tom saw that the pair had stopped at a high, sheer rock face. Kensa seemed to be inspecting it carefully. Tom saw Jeng lower himself onto a reddish rock, his shoulders slumping in exhaustion. Tom and Elenna crept closer.

"What are they doing?" Elenna whispered.

"I don't know," Tom replied. "But

they've walked into a dead end. We should strike now, while they're trapped."

"They'll hear us coming," Elenna warned. "Kensa will use her Lightning Staff against us."

As she spoke, Tom saw Kensa reach into her cloak and pull out a glass vial. They watched the witch dip her finger into the container like it was an inkwell and draw something on the cliff face.

A five-pointed star.

A brilliant flash of light lit the sombre scene and they watched Jeng slide off the rock, cowering behind it as the rock face began to shimmer.

"A portal!" Tom cried. "Quick,

they'll get away! We have to go now!"

They scrambled down the slope as fast as they could. As he ran, Tom saw Kensa and Jeng pass through the glowing portal, disappearing in an instant. Immediately, the portal began to shrink. Tom sprinted harder, clattering over loose rocks despite the risk. *We have to follow them through.*

"Run, Elenna!" he cried. They were twenty paces away, now ten, but the portal had nearly closed. They weren't going to make it. Unless… Tom stopped and grabbed Elenna as she caught up. He held her tightly, crouched and leapt towards the closing portal, which was now hardly big enough to fit one person, let alone two. He knew he needed to judge it perfectly, or else…

Tom and Elenna shot through the

tiny gap. The world went black as Tom felt a sickening, lurching sensation… but it was over in a second, and they were on the other side, tumbling onto hot, dusty earth.

Coughing and groaning, Tom sat up. He blinked at Elenna through the blinding light. She lay in the dust. Tom scrambled over and helped her up.

"Are you all right?" Tom asked.

Elenna nodded. "Just a mouthful of dust," she croaked.

It's not dust, it's sand! Tom thought. *Where has the portal taken us?* From the freezing, snow-covered wastelands of Vareen, they'd suddenly found themselves in a hot, dry land. Tom stood up and looked around, squinting in the dazzling light. There was no sign of Kensa or Jeng. Tom saw nothing but a flat expanse of sand, with just a few

scraggly plants and an occasional sick-looking cactus. There was nowhere to hide.

"Where are we?" Elenna asked,

dusting herself off.

"No idea," Tom replied with a frown. "We have no map, no water and no landmarks."

He turned slowly to take it in. All around, the desert stretched in every direction as far as the eye could see. He could already feel the fierce heat of the sun through his clothes. The thin shriek of a vulture made him look up and he saw the bird wheeling above. A creeping dread came over him.

"Elenna... I'm starting to wonder if we've walked right into a trap."

THE PEOPLE OF THE DESERT

"What should we do, Tom?" Elenna asked, fear in her voice.

Tom had no answer. His hand automatically went to the pouch on his belt, but he couldn't see any way the two shards of the Broken Star could help them just now. The vulture shrieked again and Tom looked up to see that the bird had moved off towards the horizon.

What has it found that's more interesting than us?

Tom summoned the power of the golden helmet once more and peered in the direction the bird was heading. There was a dark smudge, far in the distance. He squinted and tried to make out what it was: a sliver of green cutting through the otherwise featureless plain. His heart surged with hope.

"I can see something," Tom said. "It could be an oasis."

"Or a mirage," Elenna replied.

"We might as well look," Tom pointed out. Elenna nodded in

agreement, and they set off across the burning sands. They walked in silence. Tom could feel the intense heat of the sand through the soles of his boots and the burn of the sun creeping through his tunic.

"How are you doing?" he croaked to Elenna.

"Surviving...just about," Elenna said thickly. He turned to look at her. Her lips were swollen and cracked and her face was burnt red. Tom took off his undershirt and tore it in half, fashioning head cloths to offer them both some protection. Then they carried on plodding. It was slow going, with loose sand shifting under their every step.

Tom soon lost track of time and kept his head down, seeing nothing but the sand right in front of him. His vision grew hazy and he wondered if he was seeing things

when a patch of grass came into view. He stumbled and fell to his knees, his vision swimming. A single white flower stood up within the clump. He hauled himself to his feet and carried on. But then there was another patch of grass, and another. Then more flowers.

"Tom!" Elenna croaked. He looked up and saw that she was pointing ahead. He turned to see.

The oasis!

Tom's heart surged as he took in the rich jumble of plant life. He saw bushes, grass, flowers, coconuts and fruit trees. Right in the middle of the oasis lay a small lake, shimmering in the gentle breeze. A rickety old pier stretched out into deeper water. From somewhere Tom found the strength to run, Elenna right behind him. He dropped his sword and shield, raced down the jetty and dived into the cool lake. He imagined he heard the hiss as the water touched his burning skin. He drank in little sips, turning and laughing when he saw Elenna up to her ears in the pool, gulping down the cool, fresh water. But his laughter died when a voice cut across it.

"You two seem to be a long way from home."

Tom's heart leapt into his mouth as he looked up to see a crowd of people had appeared by the lake – men and women, even children. Behind the group stood a number of camels, snorting and pulling at their reins. Though the children were smiling, Tom thought some of the men seemed to be looking at him with mistrust. His eyes flicked over to where he'd dropped his sword and shield on the bank.

How did they manage to sneak up like that?

"Do not be concerned," one of the men said, stepping forward. He seemed to be an elder, dressed in long robes and with a full white beard and kind eyes. "The oasis is a place of peace, and here for all to use. Where have you two come from?"

Tom and Elenna trudged up the bank out of the water and stood before the man, dripping. "We are travellers from a faraway land," Tom said. His glance flickered towards the other tribespeople standing behind

the elder. He particularly noticed two tattooed men who whispered together, never taking their suspicious eyes off Tom and Elenna. Tom shot his friend a look and saw her give a slight nod. It would be safer if they didn't reveal the details

of their Quest just now. Even if these people could be trusted, he didn't want to cause panic. "Our camels ran off with our food and water. We were lucky to find this place."

"Indeed, you were," the man said. "My name is Tyroll. We will offer you food and safe passage through our territory. Come."

Tom knew that even if the villagers were no threat, Kensa and Jeng may be nearby. "Have you seen any other strangers passing through recently?" he asked Tyroll. "A man in a cloak, and a woman wearing robes?"

Tyroll answered quickly. "We have seen no one."

Tom shook his head, puzzled.

Where could they be? Tom and Elenna followed the man as he led them through the trees to the far side of the oasis to a village consisting mostly of large tents, and a few small mud huts.

"Tyroll seems friendly enough," Tom whispered to Elenna. "But some of the others appear guarded…"

"We should remain watchful," Elenna whispered back.

Tyroll invited them into his tent, the largest, in the middle of the village. There they were offered a change of clothes while they let their wet things dry.

"When you are ready, come and join us for food around the fire," Tyroll

said. Then he left them alone while they changed.

"This is too good to be true," Elenna whispered from where she was changing behind a screen.

"I agree," Tom said. "And I'm

worried that we've lost Kensa and Jeng."

When they were ready they emerged, following the delicious scent of meat roasting on charcoal braziers. The day was cooler now as the sun dropped in the sky and a pleasant breeze rustled through the trees. Tyroll greeted them and had them sit down while plates of food were brought, piled high. There were large skewers of spiced meat atop mounds of vegetables.

Tom's stomach rumbled, reminding him he hadn't eaten for ages. As he began his meal, he thought he'd never tasted anything so good in his life. Elenna grinned at him, her mouth full, clearly enjoying the food as much as he was. When they'd eaten their fill, they lay back, tummies full. Tyroll came to sit with them, a young boy in his arms.

"This is my son, Jobi," Tyroll said. Jobi seemed fascinated by the strangers, especially Elenna, who delighted the boy by showing him a clapping game. As Tom relaxed he glanced over to the other side of the fire where some of the tribespeople were involved in a strange activity. They were bending and grabbing handfuls of sand, before rising, holding their arms high and letting the sand slide through their fingers. An old woman tossed a handful of dust into the fire and Tom smelled the thick, sweet scent of incense.

"It is a ritual," Tyroll explained. "This is the season when we make offerings to Okko."

"Okko?" Tom asked, curious.

"The sand monster," Tyroll explained. "If we fail to appease him, he punishes us with sandstorms."

Tom sat up. "This sand monster… what does he look like?"

"A great Beast, made of sand. It is said that he is as taller than the highest dune, with eyes as deep as wells and arms as long as palm trees."

"Have you seen him?" Tom asked. If Okko was real, and not just a campfire tale, then he might be the

Beast who was guarding the third fragment of the Broken Star. Perhaps they weren't as far from the Quest as Tom had feared.

"No one has seen him for generations," Tyroll said. "He lives to the North and he hates people encroaching on his territory. We stay away."

"I have heard him, though," Jobi said, fearfully. "I left the village one night, looking for my pet goat who ran away. I went too far and heard Okko roaring in the desert."

Tyroll laughed. "That was just the wind." But the boy shook his head and ran to his mother on the other side of the campfire.

"The goat didn't run away," Tyroll said, quietly so the boy wouldn't hear. "We send animals north from time to time. As sacrifices. None return." Tom felt an icy chill creep up his back.

He sat back, putting thoughts of sand monsters out of his mind. As he stared into the fire he felt a thick drowsiness wash over him. He saw Elenna's head dropping too. He blinked and shook his head to clear it. *Perhaps it's the incense.* The two tattooed men he'd seen whispering together earlier were sitting directly opposite them, watching intently – as if waiting for something. He looked over to Elenna and noticed her eyes had closed. Tom roused himself and nudged her awake.

"I think we need to go," he muttered to her. "We can't let Jeng and Kensa get too much of a head-start."

Elenna stretched groggily and nodded in agreement.

"Thank you for your hospitality," Tom said to Tyroll, his head feeling like it was full of cotton. "But my friend and I must keep moving."

"Now?" Tyroll said in surprise. "But night is falling. Where would you go?"

"North," Tom said firmly.

Tyroll rose to his feet. "Madness! Did you not hear me tell you that nothing ever returns alive from the North?"

"Nonetheless, we must try," Tom said.

"At least wait until morning." Tyroll's voice sounded desperate. "Only a fool would travel across the freezing desert at night."

Tom shook his head and took a step towards the tent where they'd left their own clothes. But the tattooed men suddenly appeared and blocked his path. Tom was about to demand that they step aside when he heard Elenna scream behind him. He spun round, only to find the light blacked out as someone behind him thrust a rough canvas bag over his head.

Tom struggled but many hands grabbed firm hold of him. He felt his wrists tied firmly behind his back.

Then he heard Tyroll call for quiet amidst the voices.

"We know who you are," he said, all trace of friendship drained from his voice. "Traitors to the kingdom!"

Tom felt himself manhandled and pushed along for a few dozen steps. Unable to see, his hearing suddenly seemed stronger. He caught the heavy breathing of his guards, the sound of Elenna's feet stumbling along behind him, and the sound of the palm trees rustling in the desert breeze. They walked for some time through soft sand until Tom was shoved roughly to his knees. The sack was torn off and Tom looked up to see a familiar, and most unwelcome,

figure towering above him.

"Tom! Elenna!" cried Emperor Jeng. "We meet again!"

3 CAPTIVES

They were in a tent that was even bigger than Tyroll's and lavishly decorated with red velvet and tasselled rugs. Golden pots and plates of exquisite workmanship hung from the walls. A table covered with silver plates of rich food stood in the centre of the tent.

"Thank you for bringing the

Avantian to me," Jeng said, taking a bite from a chicken leg. He planted a foot on Tom's shoulder and kicked him over so that he sprawled on the rug.

"Tom is a friend of Gwildor," Elenna said. "Son of your Mistress of Beasts." But if Elenna had thought this might get a sympathetic response, she was wrong. Tyroll spat at his feet.

"What is Freya to us?" he demanded. "She has never dared venture this far north to face the sand monster. But here, in our village, is the emperor himself, who has promised gold and livestock for us to offer as sacrifices."

Jeng smiled at him. "I have nothing but respect for my hardy subjects of the North who stand alone against the fearsome Okko."

The villagers nodded at this and Tom could only shake his head at the nerve of the emperor. "Now, good people," Jeng went on. "If I might be granted some time alone with the captives to question them?"

Tyroll agreed and led his men out through the tent flap. Tom took a deep breath and tried to break out of his bonds. But even using the magic from his golden breastplate, he could not free himself.

"Kensa's work," said Jeng, leering down at him. "Before she set off, she gifted the villagers with some special rope from Henkrall. It's as tough as steel!"

"Speaking of the witch, where is

Kensa?" Tom asked. "It's unlike you to do anything without her telling you to."

"Kensa has gone north, to face the sand monster and take his star fragment," Jeng replied.

"No surprise that you were too cowardly to go with her," Elenna said scathingly.

Jeng shrugged off the insult. "Why bother to walk across a desert to fight a Beast when two star fragments are following me around? Now, please allow me to relieve you of the burden of carrying them any longer. They must be so heavy."

Jeng crossed the carpet, and with a quick movement tugged the pouch away from Tom's belt. Tom stretched and twisted, trying to break free, but was powerless to stop the theft. He groaned inwardly. *After all we've been through to win those fragments…*

Jeng laughed and held out one hand, palm up. He tipped the pouch over it and shook out…

Two smooth stones!

Jeng stared in astonishment, as did Tom. Looking over at Elenna he nearly laughed to see her wink at him. Somehow she must have switched the fragments with the stones. But when?

Jeng howled in fury. "What have you done with them?"

Tom shrugged. He honestly had no idea where they were. Jeng crossed quickly to the smoking charcoal brazier and pulled from it a wicked-looking, long skewer, glowing hot from the coals.

"I'll make you tell me where the fragments are," he growled.

Tom swallowed nervously as Jeng

took a step towards Elenna. "She knows nothing," Tom cried. "I hid the fragments, not her."

"Oh, I don't doubt that," Jeng said, sneering. "That's why I intend to use this on her instead of you. That way you'll be sure to talk." He took another step towards Elenna, whose eyes widened with fear.

"Don't tell him anything, Tom," she said.

But before Jeng could take another step, Tom heard cries of alarm and a howling, crackling sound. Sand blew into the tent and Tom turned away to shield his eyes. One of the tribesmen rushed in and fell to his knees, sobbing with fear.

"It is Okko," the man cried. "We have displeased him."

The roar of the wind outside grew louder. Through narrowed eyes Tom watched Jeng drop the skewer and fall backwards in fear as the entire tent was suddenly lifted by the wind. Tom heard the popping of tent pegs as they were ripped from the ground leaving them exposed to the howling elements. Tom could hardly keep his eyes open as the stinging sand flew into them, but he forced himself to squint. He'd seen something which gave him hope. *The skewer!*

The whistling wind had caused it to glow white hot and it had set fire to a section of the expensive rug. Tom managed to get to his feet, rushed over to the fire and knelt down. Kensa's rope might have been impervious to his strength, but would it stand up to flames? Tom held the bonds as close as he could until he felt the rope strands split. Fire licked his arms and he fought the urge to pull back from the agonising pain. He knew this was his only chance.

Tom looked up to see Jeng climbing to his feet. "Guards!" the emperor called, only for the words to be whipped from his mouth by the roar of the wind.

Yanking his hands apart, Tom broke the last strands of the rope.

He stood and charged Jeng with his shoulder, knocking him over again. Tom seized another burning skewer from the brazier and held it over Jeng. "I could kill you – but I show

you the mercy you did not show to my mother."

Jeng said nothing, but just stared back at Tom, his face full of fear and hate.

Keeping the skewer pointed at Jeng, Tom used his free hand to help Elenna with her bonds. The wind was as strong as ever and his eyes stung with gritty sand, making his job even harder.

"Hurry, Tom," Elenna cried. "The fire – it's spreading!"

1

A STRANDED ENEMY

Tom turned to see that the fire was heading towards them across the floor rugs. He took a deep breath, tugging harder at Elenna's bonds, freeing her just as he felt the heat of the fire on his feet.

Together they ran from the remains of the tent. Shielding their eyes from the stinging sand, they passed tribespeople wailing in fear. A woman saw them and clutched her child to her chest, her eyes large with terror. What had Jeng told them to make them so fearful? But there was no time to stop and find out.

Tom made to head out of the village, but Elenna pulled him back.

"We need to go back to Tyroll's tent," she cried against the wind.

"There's no time," Tom said. "Jeng will send men after us."

"I left something important there," Elenna explained, leading him back to Tyroll's tent. It was sagging in the wind, but still mostly upright. They dived inside and Elenna showed him where she'd hidden the two star fragments, behind the screen, when she was changing her clothes.

"That was brilliant thinking," Tom said, grinning. "You might just have saved Gwildor."

They left the tent and slipped hurriedly through the village towards the lake. Hiding in the undergrowth, they waited while the wind died down. In time, the relentless patter of sand against the leaves was replaced by a gentle hush as the first pinkish flecks of dawn crept up over the horizon. Tom watched the villagers return and try to repair the damage the storm had caused. He saw Jeng, looking self-assured now that the danger had passed.

"Find those traitors and kill them on sight," he roared.

So much for mercy, Tom thought. *It might be a good idea for us to get away from the village now.*

A snorting noise from behind startled him. He spun to see two camels – one watching him curiously, the other drinking from the lake.

"They must have been freed during the storm," Tom said. He was pleased to see each had a water flask dangling from its saddle. He reached up and stroked the first camel's nose, then grinned mischievously at Elenna.

"I've never ridden a camel before," he said.

"Me neither," Elenna replied.

The saddles had stirrups, and getting up onto the camels' backs was straightforward enough, but they proved to be skittish creatures. Tom was worried their huffs and grunts would draw the attention of the villagers, so he urged his camel into a swift trot, directly away from the village. They followed the trail of destruction the storm had made. Cacti had been torn up and the sand was disturbed.

Tom looked at the position of the sun to calculate what direction they were headed in. He wasn't surprised to find it was due north. Had Okko sent the storm? They rode on, sweating as the unforgiving sun poured its heat over them.

"I think we might have company,"

Elenna said after a while. Tom turned to see dots on the horizon, behind them. Tom summoned the power of the golden helmet to get a better view.

"Camel riders," he said.

"Tribespeople from the village."
Tom spurred his camel on and saw Elenna beside him doing the same.

After a while he turned to see that their pursuers had dropped back. Even at this great distance, the magic of the helmet allowed him to see the expressions on their faces. "They look fearful," he went on. "I get the feeling they don't want to travel so far north, despite Jeng's orders."

"I think I can guess why," Elenna said, pointing. Tom turned to see a pile of animal skeletons, jumbled together as though they been thrown there.

"Did they die of thirst, do you

think?" Elenna asked.

"They wouldn't be piled up like this if they did," Tom replied. "I think these animals were eaten."

As they rode on, they passed more skeleton piles, bones bleached white by the relentless sun. *Something out here has a great hunger.*

"Riding a camel certainly beats walking," Tom said, trying to take his mind off the skeletons.

"Yes, it does!" Elenna agreed, taking a swig of water.

Tom's camel grunted and shook its head, as if it sensed approaching danger. Tom stroked its neck. "Sorry. We can't turn back now." He swallowed nervously as he wondered just what kind of creature had left this litter of bleached bones behind.

"What's that?" Elenna cried, pointing ahead. Tom squinted against the glare. Elenna had good eyes, even without a magical helmet to help! Something lay on the desert sands. It looked like a pile of rags...

Or a body?

As they approached, he realised the second guess was right. There was someone lying amidst the animal bones. *Kensa!*

"This could be a trap," Elenna warned.

Tom nodded and got down off his camel, handing the reins to Elenna.

He drew his sword. The sharp sound seemed to wake Kensa and she looked up at them. Her face was horribly sunburnt, and Tom could see her cracked lips moving but no sound came out. She stared at Tom

through bloodshot eyes, with no trace of recognition.

This was no trap. Tom sheathed his sword and rushed back to the camel, grabbing the flask. He raced back to Kensa and crouched down beside her again. Lifting her head carefully, he tipped a little of the precious water between her parched lips. Kensa drank it down gratefully.

"Kensa," Tom said. "What happened?"

She fixed him with a stare full of madness and fear.

"Okko," she said. "He has come."

Tom stood and scanned the horizon. There was no sign of any Beast – just the desert, just the bones. He was about to reassure Kensa when he felt his legs buckle. The ground beneath his feet had shifted…

"What is it, Tom?" Elenna cried in alarm. The camels were grunting and groaning in fear.

Tom tried to answer but choked as a great cloud of sand was thrown up around him. Tom froze in horror as he watched the sand cloud solidify and form itself into the shape of a huge four-fingered hand. The great fingers cupped around him, gripped him tightly and thrust him upwards.

Half-blinded, Tom screamed in terror as the giant hand began squeezing the life out of him.

BREATHLESS

Fighting for breath, Tom watched the ground drop away as more of Okko's form emerged from the ground, lifting him higher. The Beast's grip loosened slightly and Tom snatched a painful breath. He saw Kensa thrown to one side below, and Elenna struggling to keep the camels under control. Then

he was spun around and he got his first good look at the Beast. Okko's face was still forming from a cloud of loose sand. Tom saw a jutting nose and a cavernous mouth filled with rocky stumps of teeth. Last to form were the great hollow eye sockets, like bottomless wells in the sandy skull.

Tom's right arm was squeezed against his side but he found he was able to shift his hand just enough to touch the red jewel in his belt that allowed him to talk to Beasts.

I am a friend, he told Okko. *I am here to help you fight our mutual enemies. Kensa and—*

Tom couldn't finish his thought, because he was blasted by Okko's sandy breath, which hit his face like a thousand needles, flaying his skin. Then the blast stopped as the

Beast's mouth closed.

I bow to no one. Okko's voice was a cruel rasp in Tom's mind. Then the Beast opened his great, gaping mouth to blast Tom again. This time he'd be shredded, he knew it.

Desperately, Tom wrenched an arm free, drew his sword and swung the blade, cutting deeply into the back of the Beast's hand. Tom's stomach lurched as he found himself falling through the air. Okko had dropped him as he recoiled in pain. Tom screamed as he fell, but quickly found himself snatched out of the air by Okko's other hand.

The breath was forced out of his

lungs as the giant fingers squeezed tight, pinning Tom's arms to his sides. But Okko hadn't counted on the power of the golden breastplate. Forcing his arms outwards, Tom broke the crushing grip of the sand monster and leapt out into thin air, trusting in the power of Arcta's eagle feather to break his fall. But, again, Okko caught him as he fell. The Beast gave voice to a curious, deep-throated noise and Tom realised Okko was laughing.

He's toying with me! Tom thought. *Like a cat with a mouse.*

Down below he saw Elenna had gathered her bow and arrows and was bracing herself to take a shot.

But Okko opened his mouth and roared. Tom saw Elenna blasted backwards.

Holding Tom by the ankles, the Beast swung him back and forth.

Tom watched in despair as his sword and shield fell to the ground far below. He groaned as the blood rushed to his head. Elenna had stepped forwards again and was tracking Okko with an arrow.

"Shoot!" Tom cried in desperation.

"I can't get a clear shot," Elenna cried. "I might hit you."

"You won't!" Tom shouted as he watched Okko's mouth opening again to blast Elenna once more. "Do it!" He heard the twang of the bow string, the hiss of the arrow and the howl from Okko as the arrow sank into his upper arm. Tom felt the wind whistle through his hair as he was dropped again, tumbling head over heels.

Okko roared angrily and swatted Elenna with his club-like fist. Tom watched in horror as her limp body flew through the air and landed in a heap, not moving. He saw Kensa crawling away. *Trying to save her own skin,* he thought angrily. Now it was just him and the Beast. A shadow fell across him and he looked up to see Okko raising a fist. Realising what was about to happen, Tom took a huge lungful of air and shut his eyes as the fist came down like a pile-driver, hammering him deep into the shifting sand.

Everything went dark. Tom was buried under the crushing weight of the desert sand. He kept his eyes tightly shut, lying trapped and blind. He heard nothing but the pounding of his heart, and felt nothing but the sickening terror in his gut. He was still alive...but for how long?

TRIBE IN DANGER

Tom's burning lungs urged him to draw breath, but he knew if he tried he'd choke on sand. A dull sense of defeat crept over him and he felt his body shutting down, giving up.

But then something shifted above him, a slight lessening of the weight. He thrust upwards with the last of his strength and felt a hand grab his wrist, hauling him out of the sand into the daylight. He took a huge, shuddering breath, the dry desert atmosphere tasting like the sweetest mountain air. Brushing sand out of

his eyes, he opened them to see the concerned face of Elenna looking back at him.

"You're alive!" he cried, embracing his friend. "I thought…I thought…"

"Okko thought the same," Elenna replied with a grin. "I had to play dead until he left."

"Where did he go?"

"Towards the oasis," Elenna said grimly. "And he's moving quickly. I think he means business."

Tom stood groggily and peered around for the camels, but they were nowhere to be seen. The two friends collected their weapons and headed back towards the oasis on foot. They hadn't gone far when a sudden movement caught their eye. A figure darted out from behind a low dune, running directly away from them. Tom recognised the Lightning Staff that she carried.

"Kensa," Elenna said, notching an arrow and firing it past the witch's head, close enough to let her know the next one wouldn't be just a warning. Kensa stopped and turned, holding up her hands in surrender as Tom and Elenna trudged towards her. Tom felt the sun beat down mercilessly on the back of his neck as he approached the witch. He could see she was terrified.

"It's time you started making amends for the damage you've

caused," Tom told her. "Help us get back to the oasis."

"Are you mad?" Kensa asked. "That's where Okko is headed. Jeng can fend for himself."

"It's not Jeng I'm concerned about," Tom said. "It's the tribespeople. Just because Jeng lied to them doesn't mean we should abandon them to Okko."

"I won't do it," Kensa said. "It's too dangerous. Besides, I'm not even sure I have the strength."

"Perhaps this will give you the energy boost you need," Tom said, drawing his sword with a scrape of steel.

"Or this?" Elenna added, raising

her bow. Kensa glared at them, but there was genuine fear in her eyes. She clearly believed Tom and Elenna were prepared to kill her if she refused to help. With a grimace, Kensa hefted her Lightning Staff and drew a circle in the sand. In the circle, she drew a five-pointed star, then muttered some words under her breath. As Tom watched, the portal immediately began to shimmer like the one they'd seen earlier in the stone wall.

"Looks like you had more strength than you thought," Tom said. Then he shoved her towards the portal.

"What are you doing?" Kensa cried out in horror.

"Making sure it's safe," Tom said. "If there's a nasty surprise on the other side, you'll have to deal with it first." With a wail, Kensa disappeared from view. Tom and Elenna glanced at each other before following her through the portal.

But to where?

Tom was relieved to find they had emerged back at the oasis, just outside the village. There appeared to be no sign of Okko. Kensa hobbled quickly towards Jeng's tent, which seemed to have been mostly rebuilt.

Seeing her, one of the tribesmen cried out a warning and within seconds they were surrounded by armed men and women, including the fierce men with tattoos. A breeze rustled through the palms, cooling Tom's forehead. But he couldn't help feeling a flicker of fear as he noticed that it came from the North.

"You are in great danger," Tom said. "Okko is coming."

"If so, it is because you have angered him," one of the men shouted.

Then Tom saw Jeng storming over. The breeze had picked up and the tent flap flicked back and forth behind him. Kensa was nowhere to be seen.

"Shall I run him through?" One of the tattooed men grabbed Tom's arm in a fierce grip.

Jeng raised a hand. "Not just yet," he said. "Tom may prove useful."

"Okko is coming," Tom repeated slowly. "You should leave the village now. Or at least prepare to fight."

"Lies," Jeng spat. "We sent a sacrifice north just yesterday. Okko will not come here."

"Ask Kensa if you don't believe us," Elenna said. "Why do you think she ran? She saw the Beast."

"Kensa is resting after her ordeal," Jeng replied. "After you attacked her, that is."

Tom shook his head in despair. *What is Jeng playing at? Can he not see the danger? Unless...*

"You want Okko to come," Tom said as realisation dawned. "You are hoping we will defeat him so you can take the fragment. And if we die in the process, then so much the better for you." More of the villagers were now looking nervous. Sand stung Tom's face as the wind whipped up further. Jeng glanced up at the palm trees, which were now beginning to bend.

"Another sandstorm?" a woman groaned.

Tom recognised Tyroll pushing his way through the crowd, his son following. Tyroll looked at Jeng first, then at Tom. Finally he turned to the North, to where a great cloud of sand had lifted from the desert and was sweeping towards them like a dirty brown tidal wave.

Tom felt the breath catch in his throat. A hubbub rose from the crowd and he felt his captor's grip loosen. There, in the centre of the storm, and covering the ground towards the oasis at an impossible speed, was the giant form of Okko. The Beast was still some distance away, but Tom could see his great mouth was open in a roar.

"Stand and fight, you cowards," Jeng commanded as the villagers began to slip away.

"And what of you?" Tyroll asked, his eyes cold. "Will you fight for our village?"

"Of course," Jeng stammered. "But I am a general, not a warrior. It is best that I fall back and...direct the troops. And first, I must check on our friend Kensa." He turned and hurried back to his tent.

"Let them go," Tyroll commanded the tattooed men who held Tom and Elenna, and they obeyed. Tom rubbed his wrists. The wind suddenly caught a tent, ripping it from its mooring. It sailed past them, causing them to duck. Tom heard someone shout in fear as the sun was blotted out by the sand cloud.

"Look, Tom," Elenna cried over the roaring wind. Tom saw that Okko

was closer now. He would reach the village in seconds. Tom drew his sword and saw Elenna notching an arrow. Looking up, he saw a few brave villagers had formed a defensive line in front of the village in a desperate effort to stop Okko.

They carried an assortment of weapons – swords, spears and slings. As Tom and Elenna rushed to join them, he saw the defenders hurling spears and Tyroll twirling a sling before releasing a sharp rock. Tyroll's rock bounced off the monster's cheek, causing nothing more than a flinch. *How can we defeat him with such puny weapons?*

Okko stopped and turned to face his attackers. Just then, Tom saw with horror that Tyroll's son, Jobi, was racing out across the sands towards his father.

There was no time to do anything but watch as Okko opened his mouth and skittled the villagers with his sandy breath. Tom heard muffled screams as the poor defenders were sent tumbling and scraping across the rough sand. Jobi escaped the worst of the blast but was quickly snatched up by Okko, who lifted the boy high and inspected him closely, just as he'd done with Tom.

Tyroll yelled with rage and snatched up a fallen spear, hurling it at Okko with all his strength. The spear buried itself deep into Okko's chest. The Beast roared and dropped the child. Tom froze in shock as he watched the boy as he plummeted, screaming, to the unforgiving ground below.

THE WEIGHT OF WATER

While the other defenders were still clambering to their feet, and Tyroll stood, frozen in horror, Tom summoned the power of the golden leg armour and raced towards Okko, arriving just in time to catch the boy before he hit the ground. Tom tumbled over, clutching the boy to

his chest to protect him, then ran back to Tyroll.

"Take him, hide yourselves," Tom gasped as Elenna arrived. "Help them, Elenna. I'll deal with Okko."

"How?" Tyroll exclaimed, accepting his son from Tom and hugging him tight.

Behind them, Okko had lumbered into the village and was busy ripping up tents and smashing the wooden huts with his powerful fists. The huge Beast seemed to be scanning the ground, perhaps looking for a new plaything.

"I have a plan," Tom told him. "Sort of."

With that, he turned and sprinted

back through the village, dodging Okko as the Beast tried to grab him again. As he'd hoped, the sand monster followed, roaring in anger. Tom headed towards the oasis, but not so fast as to discourage Okko from his pursuit.

I have to give the villagers enough time to escape.

He turned to make sure Okko was following and saw the Beast blasting tents with his breath and tearing up trees with his huge hands. He was getting closer. Tom skidded down the muddy bank of the oasis, and tried to hide himself in a clump of reeds by the water's edge. His heart was pounding, his lungs burning. Okko emerged from the tall trees and stopped, looking around.

Looking for me.

Tom peered out from between two clumps of reeds as Okko scanned the water's edge. Then the Beast opened his mouth. Tom flinched as

Okko unleashed another blast of his baking hot breath. Tom cowered and winced as flecks of flying sand tore into his exposed flesh. The blast ended and he looked up in alarm to see the reeds had been flattened, revealing his hiding place. Okko came storming down the bank and raised his leg, ready to stomp. Tom rolled clear as the Beast's heel splashed down in the muddy shallows, sinking into the soft bank.

As Tom tried to get to his feet, he was surprised to see Okko's leg seemed to be stuck in the mud. The Beast grunted with the effort of wrenching it free and Tom saw the dirty brown sand of his foot had turned black, like caked mud.

Of course! Wet sand became heavy sand. *If I can just get him into the oasis, he won't be able to move as quickly. I might have half a chance!*

Okko came after him again, but Tom now had a speed advantage. He ran along the shore to the spindly jetty and ran down it, light on his feet. He stopped at the very end and turned back to face his pursuer. Okko roared in anger at Tom's lack of fear, taking two long strides along the jetty...

Yes! It's working...

The Beast stopped. He glanced down, clearly aware that the splintered planks wouldn't hold his

weight. He looked up at Tom, the great hollows of his eyes seeming to narrow. He was judging the distance. Tom took a few steps back towards his foe. *Follow me. Follow me!*

When Tom was just a dozen paces away, Okko lifted his right arm. Quick as the wind, the arm stretched out, impossibly long, and seized Tom once again. Okko dragged Tom back down the jetty and lifted the hero towards his yawning mouth. Tom saw up close the Beast's huge teeth, jutting like cracked paving slabs. He had a sudden flashback to the bleached bones in the desert. Okko intended to eat him alive!

With a last, desperate show of strength, Tom wrenched his sword arm free and slashed at Okko's face, carving a great gash in the monster's cheek. Okko flinched and for a split second loosened his grip. Tom took his chance and sprang clear of the great sandy fingers. As he fell, Tom twisted, and held his shield above him, trusting in the power of the eagle feather to slow his fall.

But nothing happened. He plummeted hard and crashed through the jetty, smashing the half-rotten planks and crunching into the river bank below. He landed horribly, his left leg twisted underneath him. Tom felt the bone snap and a wave of agony swept through him. For a second he almost blacked out. Why hadn't the power of the feather broken his fall? Tom reached for his shield, turning it over to examine it.

Oh, no...

His chest tightened with dread when he saw that the six tokens he had won on his earliest Beast Quests had somehow been drained

of all their colour. *How did that happen?*

Then he remembered his previous Quest, when Thoron's lightning hit his shield during battle. *Did that somehow robbed my tokens of their magic?*

Tom lay and looked up through the hole his body had punched in the jetty. The light was soon blocked by Okko's head, leering down at him. Tom heard the Beast's taunt through his red jewel. *You are defeated. I will return to kill you once I have dealt with the archer girl.*

Then he was gone. Tom pulled the green jewel from his belt – the jewel that healed injuries. He held it against his broken leg and felt the bone knitting as the green jewel hummed and throbbed in his hand. It was working! But suddenly he felt a powerful blow against his wrist and the jewel went flying, landing with a plop in the mud. Tom cried in pain and twisted to see Jeng standing over him with a wicked grin. He held a blade to Tom's throat – a blade he recognised.

My sword!

"You have been a worthy adversary," the evil emperor sneered. "But it's time for you to die. And by your own blade!" Jeng lifted the sword high as Tom lay helpless, waiting for the blow that would end his Beast Quest...once and for all.

VICTORY AND TREACHERY

With a grunt, Jeng brought the blade slicing down.

Thunk!

Tom stared up in amazement at the stout shaft of a spear which had appeared, apparently from nowhere, blocking Jeng's blow. *Tyroll!* The old man was glaring at Jeng. Behind him the two tattooed men stood, spears in hand.

"Fools!" Jeng hissed. "Don't you see, this is our chance to rid ourselves of an enemy of Gwildor?"

"Tom is no enemy of Gwildor," Tyroll said. "He has proved his worth. He saved my son."

"Treachery," Jeng spat. "Stand aside and let me finish the job." He thrust Tyroll's spear away and lifted his sword again. But this time the two tattooed villagers leapt to Tom's aid, one seizing Jeng and the other knocking the sword from his hand with a sharp crack of his spear butt.

"All you have done is hide from us, and lie to us," one of the men said, pressing his spear point against Jeng's chest, forcing him backwards.

"Thank you," Tom said as Tyroll extended a hand to help him up. He'd never been so grateful. "But could you please pass me that green jewel?"

Tyroll did so and Tom held it against his leg, sighing with relief as the pain eased. The wind had picked up again and the sky was darkening.

A scream from overhead caught everyone's attention and Tom looked up to see the great sandstorm cloud approaching. Within it, flung about and buffeted by the spiralling winds, was Elenna. Okko was toying with her. Tom jammed the green jewel back into his belt – his recovery would have to wait. He snatched up his sword and limped, battered and bruised, towards the Beast once more. Villagers hurled spears, which the sand monster knocked aside with his massive fists.

Tom heard Jeng groan in terror as Okko thundered towards them, poor Elenna twisting above him.

"Hey!" Tom screamed into the wind. "Down here!" He hurled his sword at Okko, the blade sinking deeply into the Beast's thigh. Okko roared and pulled the sword out. He turned to Tom and fixed him with his empty, hollow-eyed glare before hurling the sword away. Tom had a plan, and he wouldn't need his sword for it. Instead, he reached towards the pouch at his belt. As Okko's hand shot out and snatched him up one more time, Tom pulled out what he wanted, keeping his arm free to hold it high.

Okko lifted him to the skies, seeming to stretch up taller than ever. Through the red jewel Tom heard the Beast speak.

You will not survive this fall, puny human.

Tom knew he couldn't let the Beast drop him again. Not yet. He opened his palm and gazed into the heart of the second star fragment, focussing all his fear and despair into it, opening his mind, flooding the relic with emotion and energy.

A rushing noise overcame the howling of the wind and Tom opened his eyes to see water rising from the oasis like a rain that rose rather than fell. Okko stopped suddenly, as if unable to believe what he was seeing. Water was splattering up his legs, drenching his waist. He lurched backwards, trying to get away, but still the water gushed,

reaching higher and higher as the star fragment did its work.

Wherever the water touched him,

Okko turned black. His legs stopped moving as his sand became heavy and he twisted desperately from the waist, lifting his arms up high. But Okko was powerless now. The Beast's lower body sagged and crumbled from the weight of water, and Tom found himself being lowered gently to the ground. As Elenna whirled around, Tom reached out and seized her around the waist so she wouldn't fall. Together they slid down the crumbling sand mountain that had once been Okko.

The Beast's great head was the last thing to turn black and dissolve. Tom saw the lips move slowly as Okko spoke to him one last time. *I am defeated, Son of Gwildor. Take what is rightfully yours.*

And then even the Beast's head had disappeared. Tom found himself lying on a mound of wet sand – Elenna by his side – and holding the

third star fragment in his hand. The sand shifted slowly before his eyes, individual grains lifting and flying off in a swirl towards the North like a storm of tiny midges. Okko was returning to the deserts from whence he came.

Tyroll rushed over and helped Tom and Elenna to their feet. "I think you've seen the last of Okko around here," Tom told him. "And the last of the sandstorms, too."

"Then tonight, we feast," Tyroll said, his face full of joy.

Tom and Elenna exchanged grins. Finally, a chance to rest. "What about Jeng and Kensa, though?" Elenna said, dusting herself off.

"They still need to be brought to justice."

"Fear not," Tyroll said. "We have locked them in a sturdy mud hut – the only one standing that still had its roof."

"Please tell me you haven't left them unguarded inside?" Tom asked.

"Yes. There is a guard on the door..." Tyroll began, but Tom was already racing towards the hut, ignoring the pain in his leg. He reached the hut as the startled guard watched and pulled up the bar that kept it locked. He swung the door open wide.

"No..." Tom muttered.

The hut was empty, except for a

white circle and five-pointed star drawn on one wall. Kensa's portal. Tom growled in frustration as Elenna came up behind him, Tyroll and the other villagers behind her, looking astonished.

"Where could they have gone?" Tyroll asked.

"Kensa used her magic," she said. "They will already be on the hunt for the final star fragment..."

Tom turned and stepped away from the hut, his frustration turning to determination. "There'll be no feasting for us tonight," he said grimly. "This Quest is far from over."

CONGRATULATIONS, YOU HAVE COMPLETED THIS QUEST!

At the end of each chapter you were awarded a special gold coin. The QUEST in this book was worth an amazing 8 coins.

Look at the Beast Quest totem picture inside the back cover of this book to see how far you've come in your journey to become

MASTER OF THE BEASTS.

The more books you read, the more coins you will collect!

Do you want your own Beast Quest Totem?

1. Cut out and collect the coin below
2. Go to the Beast Quest website
3. Download and print out your totem
4. Add your coin to the totem

www.beastquest.co.uk/totem

8

Don't miss the next exciting Beast Quest book, SAUREX THE SILENT CREEPER!

Read on for a sneak peek...

THE ENEMIES ESCAPE

"Kensa and Jeng have escaped!" Tom stared into the mud hut where his two enemies had been imprisoned.

"But the doorway was guarded!" cried Tyroll, the elder of the village.

Elenna stood at his side, grim-faced. "Kensa must have used her magic to get them free," she said.

As she spoke, a man came bustling up. "Two camels have been stolen from the stables!" he exclaimed.

Tom and Elenna exchanged a knowing glance.

"The witch and the treacherous emperor must have taken them," said Tom. "They can't have gone far." He strode from the hut. "We'll follow them. May we take a pair of camels?"

"Of course," said Tyroll. "But you fought long and hard against Okko the Sand Monster. You cannot leave without eating first."

Tom frowned. They were running out of time on this Quest, and despair was gnawing at his heart.

Their journey across the realm of Gwildor had been gruelling – but they had fought off Beasts of ice and smoke and sand, winning three of the four shards of the Broken Star.

Irina, the kingdom's Good Witch had told them the legend of the star. Known by the people as the "gift from the sky", it had fallen to the ground in Gwildor long ago, shattering into four shards of immense power. The ancient tales told that the star fragments could control the weather – creating terrible storms, choking fog or icy winds. So a Good Witch named Clara had taken the fragments to remote corners of Gwildor, so that no villain would ever be able to wield their power. Guarded by ferocious Beasts, these fragments had lain hidden for so long that many folk had ceased believing in them.

But two people knew the legends were true: Jeng, Gwildor's wicked emperor, and the witch Kensa. They were determined to gather the fragments and use them for their wicked purposes.

Tom's battle with Okko had been fierce and savage. He could still feel the ache where his broken leg had only just been healed by the power of Skor's green jewel.

I *can't let pain and weariness stop*

me. Kensa and Jeng will use all their terrible powers to find the fourth shard of the star.

And Tom knew that even a single star fragment could do great damage in the wrong hands.

A fire had been kindled in the middle of the village. Already the chill of night was sweeping in, and many of the villagers were huddled around the flames, reaching out grateful hands against the cold.

Tom stared around the village – the simple mud huts had been smashed in his battle with Okko.

"Eat with us," Tyroll asked again. "You saved us from certain death."

"Thank you, but we can't spare

the time," Tom said sadly. A weight settled in his heart as he thought of the expanse of empty desert that surrounded this remote oasis. "Which way should we go?"

"Might the star fragments guide us?" Elenna asked.

Tom took the three crystals from his pouch and laid them on the ground. He stared down at them, willing them to give him some clue.

Nothing happened.

Tom screwed his eyes shut, desperately trying to come up with a plan to continue the Quest.

"Tom, look!" cried Elenna. He opened his eyes and saw that two of the shards were trembling in the sand, shifting towards one another.

"Those are the pieces from Gryph and Thoron," Tom said as the two shards suddenly leaped up and fused together. The third piece began to quiver too.

Tom snatched it up. "Remember what Irina told us?" he said to Elenna. "If the star joins together again it will become a deadly weapon. Even three parts could be dangerous." He pushed the third fragment into his pouch and picked up the two fused shards, handing them to Elenna.

"Keep them somewhere safe."

"Tyroll!" Anxious voices cried out from near the fire. "Something strange is happening! Bad magic!"

Tom spun around, his hand already on his sword hilt.

He saw that the tribespeople were backing away from one section of the roaring fire.

"The flames have changed colour," said Elenna as they ran forwards. In one corner of the bonfire the flames had become a curious shade of purple. "What can that mean?"

Is this Kensa's magic?

"Stay back!" Tom cried to the crowd.

But then a familiar face appeared in the flickering flames.

"It's Irina!" Tom raised his arms. "Don't be afraid," he called to the people.

"I have little time," Irina's voice rose above the crackling fire. "The fourth Beast you seek is Saurex. He is a lizard, a chameleon of great size – and he is the most deadly of the four!"

"How do we find him?" Tom asked.

"Look to the stars," Irina said. The flames guttered and spat. The face of the Good Witch melted away.

"Irina!" Tom called, staring anxiously into the fire. But she was gone. He looked at Elenna. "I'm sure she meant to tell us more."

Elenna was gazing up into the sky. She thrust her arm out, her finger pointing to a distant constellation. "Does that look like a lizard to you?" she asked.

Tom followed the line of her finger. Low on the horizon, a long cluster of stars hung over the black hills – and Elenna was right, they did seem to form the outline of a crouching lizard.

He turned to Tyroll. "That is our way ahead."

Read *Saurex the Silent Creeper* to find out what happens next!